Dear Parent:
Your child's love of reading starts here!

Every child learns to read in a different way and at his or her own speed. Some go back and forth between reading levels and read favorite books again and again. Others read through each level in order. You can help your young reader improve and become more confident by encouraging his or her own interests and abilities. From books your child reads with you to the first books he or she reads alone, there are I Can Read Books for every stage of reading:

SHARED READING
Basic language, word repetition, and whimsical illustrations, ideal for sharing with your emergent reader

BEGINNING READING
Short sentences, familiar words, and simple concepts for children eager to read on their own

READING WITH HELP
Engaging stories, longer sentences, and language play for developing readers

READING ALONE
Complex plots, challenging vocabulary, and high-interest topics for the independent reader

I Can Read Books have Introduced children to the joy of reading since 1957. Featuring award-winning authors and illustrators and a fabulous cast of beloved characters, I Can Read Books set the standard for beginning readers.

A lifetime of discovery begins with the magical words **"I Can Read!"**

Visit www.icanread.com for information
on enriching your child's reading experience.

Pinkalicious

and the Robo-Pup

For Leo
—V.K.

The author gratefully acknowledges
the artistic and editorial contributions of
Daniel Griffo and Jacqueline Resnick.

Library of Congress Control Number: 2020949332
ISBN 978-0-06-300376-7 (trade bdg.)—ISBN 978-0-06-300375-0 (pbk.)

21 22 23 24 25   LSCC   10 9 8 7 6 5 4 3 2 1
❖
First Edition

BEGINNING 1 READING

I Can Read!

Pinkalicious

and the Robo-Pup

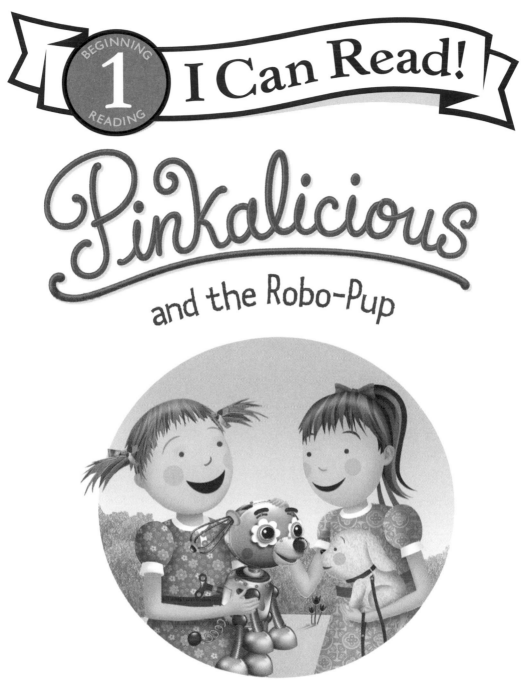

by Victoria Kann

HARPER

An Imprint of HarperCollinsPublishers

Today was Pinkville's pet contest!

"I can't wait to show everyone

our new pet," I said to Peter.

"I'm sure he'll win a trophy,"

said Peter.

We met our friends at the park.

"What kind of pet is that?"

Molly asked me.

"This is no ordinary pet," I said.

"My mom invented him
in her workshop," I told my friends.
"Robo-Pup is the perfect dog!"
said Peter.

"Robo-Pup can do tricks!"
I said proudly.
"He also barks louder, runs faster,
and has a better sense of smell
than a real dog."

My friends weren't listening.

They were too busy petting

Alison's new puppy.

"Her name is Bella," Alison said.

"Bella is so cute!" Molly said.

"Robo-Pup is great, too!" I said.

"Look what he can do.

Shake hands!" I told Robo-Pup.

He sat and gave me his paw.

"Speak!" Peter said to Robo-Pup.

"Woof, woof!" he barked.

My friends didn't pay attention.

"Awww, look at Bella wag her tail!"
Jade said.

No one cared how great Robo-Pup was!

I gave Robo-Pup a hug.

Suddenly I heard Mr. Swizzle's voice
on the loudspeaker.

"Let the contest begin!" he said.

"It's time to walk your pets

for the judges to see!"

14

Everyone cheered.

All the noise spooked Bella!

She tugged on her leash.

She broke free!

"Come back, Bella!" Alison yelled.

Bella kept running.

She bumped into dogs and cats.

She tipped over a fishbowl.

"We have to stop Bella!" I said.

"Catch that puppy!" Peter yelled.

The contest came to a halt
as everyone ran after Bella,
but she was too fast to catch.
She ran behind some trees
and disappeared.

"I don't see Bella anywhere,"
Peter said.

"How am I going to find her?"
Alison asked.

She started to cry.

"I know!" I said.

I let Robo-Pup smell Bella's toy.

"Robo-Pup is a super sniffer."

"He can find Bella!

"Go, Robo-Pup!" I commanded.

Robo-Pup sniffed his way

through the park.

He went faster and faster.

Soon he was running at super-speed!

"Wow." Molly gasped.

"He's the fastest dog

I've ever seen!"

"He's just a blur," Jade said in awe.

"I hope he finds Bella," Alison said.

Robo-Pup barked extra loudly.

"Follow that bark!" I said.

We ran after Robo-Pup.

"There he is!" Molly said.

Robo-Pup was sitting

in front of a bush.

"WOOF! WOOF! WOOF!" he barked.

We heard a little bark

from inside the bush.

"It's Bella!" Alison said.

Alison crawled into the bush
and carried Bella out.
Everyone clapped.
"Robo-Pup to the rescue!"
Peter said.

"I'm glad Bella is okay," I said.

"Thanks to Robo-Pup!" Alison said.

She gave my dog a hug.

"Thank you, Robo-Pup," she said.

"You saved my dog—

and now the contest can go on!"

As I walked with Robo-Pup,

people cheered and waved at us.

He was a hero!

"Great job, Robo-Pup!" a dad yelled.

"I want a Robo-Pup!" a girl begged.

"Me too!" said a little boy.

I spotted Mommy and Daddy.

"Way to go, Pinkalicious!"

Mommy called out.

"It's time to give out trophies!"
said Mr. Swizzle.

Alison squeezed my hand.

"The trophy for cutest puppy

goes to BELLA!" said Mr. Swizzle.

Mr. Swizzle gave a lot of trophies,

but none was for Robo-Pup.

"I'm sorry, Robo-Pup," I said sadly.

"I know how great you are,"

said Peter.

Robo-Pup wagged his tail.

Then Mr. Swizzle said,

"We have another award this year.

The biggest hero is ROBO-PUP!

Ice cream for everyone!"

"Go, Robo-Pup!" everyone cheered.

"Congratulations!" Daddy said.

"Now everyone wants

their own Robo-Pup," Mommy said.

The next week, Alison and I
took our dogs for a walk.
"I can't believe it," I said.
"Pinkville is robo-rrific!"
"Woof, woof!" barked Robo-Pup.